THE
GODDAUGHTER

THE GODDAUGHTER

MELODIE CAMPBELL

RAVEN BOOKS
an imprint of
ORCA BOOK PUBLISHERS

Library and Archives Canada Cataloguing in Publication

Campbell, Melodie, 1955-
The goddaughter / Melodie Campbell.
(Rapid reads)

Issued also in electronic formats.
ISBN 978-1-4598-0125-7

I. Title. II. Series: Rapid reads
PS8605.A54745G63 2012   C813'.6   C2012-902256-X

First published in the United States, 2012
Library of Congress Control Number: 2012938155

Summary: A young gemologist, who happens to be related to the local
mob, is reluctantly recruited to smuggle diamonds across the border…
with hilarious consequences. (RL 2.8)

*Orca Book Publishers is dedicated to preserving the environment and has
printed this book on paper certified by the Forest Stewardship Council®.*

Orca Book Publishers gratefully acknowledges the support for
its publishing programs provided by the following agencies:
the Government of Canada through the Canada Book Fund and the
Canada Council for the Arts, and the Province of British Columbia
through the BC Arts Council and the Book Publishing Tax Credit.

Design by Teresa Bubela
Cover photography by Getty Images

ORCA BOOK PUBLISHERS
PO Box 5626, Stn. B
Victoria, BC Canada
V8R 6S4

ORCA BOOK PUBLISHERS
PO Box 468
Custer, WA USA
98240-0468

www.orcabook.com
Printed and bound in Canada.

15 14 13 12 • 4 3 2 1

Dedicated to Dad,
who taught me to love books

CHAPTER ONE

I like Pete Malone of the *Steeltown Star*, especially when he comes bearing drinks.

"Big crowd at this gig," he said, handing me a glass. "The art gallery will be pleased. Did you bring the thug from New York?"

I nearly spilled some really good scotch. "I'm doing a favor for Uncle Vince."

Pete nodded. "Figured that. You're the Goddaughter."

I struggled for something smart to say.

"Does it show?"

Pete shrugged, then smiled. "Not as much as other things. I like the dress."

Bugger. Never buy a wraparound. It won't.

We watched the gilded crowd for a while, or at least I did. Pete never took his eyes off me.

"Where is the Italian Stallion, by the way? I'd like to get a few words for the paper."

I shook my head. "You really don't want to do that. Nope...I don't recommend it."

"Vince wouldn't like it?"

It was my turn to smile. "Vince doesn't read the paper. It's your tender ears I'm thinking of. They might be shocked."

Pete laughed easily. He grabbed my arm and steered me toward the outdoor patio.

"Where are we going?" I said, with a sideways glance. Pete looked good from any angle. I like a tall man in a dark-gray suit.

"Somewhere I can speak with you in private. I never get to see you alone."

My flirt-alert went off the scale.

"Why not? Are you philosophically against calling a girl and asking her out?"

He laughed. "Now, see? That's what I like about you, Gina. Always a smart-ass."

I took a sip of scotch. "I thought you liked the way I dress."

"That too." Pete's big hand on my arm was hot. I liked his wavy honey-colored hair, and the set of his solid footballer body.

"So why haven't you picked up a phone?" I said.

"Because I'm not suicidal." He held the glass door open.

I paused a beat. "Ah. You fear the family connection. It wasn't my choice, you know. You don't get to choose your relatives."

As our feet touched the terrace, the night exploded.

"What the—?" Pete grabbed me, and we slammed to the ground. I landed on his arm.

Our drinks went flying. More shots rang out. We rolled.

The air went quiet.

Seconds later, Pete pushed away from me. He vaulted up, scanning the terrace for damage. I struggled to see through the dust. When I got to my feet, Pete was standing over a dead body.

"You fond of that guy from New York?" he said.

I took a breath. "Not so much, now that he's full of holes."

CHAPTER TWO

Pete stood guard over the body until the cops arrived. He was good at it. Crowds of haughty people in swank evening garb tried to find a way through the glass doors to peek at the carnage. Pete used his big arms to motion people back. He also frowned a lot and looked mean.

I sat down on the edge of a concrete planter and tried to remain calm. It was a beautiful May night, softly warm and just a tiny bit humid.

But three bullets and a river of blood can mess up a girl's composure. After all,

I did arrive at this gala with the man on the ground...I was even related to him, in a completely depressing way. You might even consider that he had been in my care, in so much as he was a guest of my Uncle Vince. This was just not a good train of thought. It led one to contemplate other distressing things. Such as—what the hell was going on, and why didn't I know about it?

Ten minutes later, the cops were in control, and we were seated in the art gallery's swish boardroom. The black leather chair swallowed me up. We were surrounded by lavish paintings that graced the dove-gray walls. Pete kept me company as we waited to be questioned. He seemed to think I needed comforting, or maybe even protecting. I like that in a non-relative.

I was deep in thought, gazing at the floor. So, apparently, was Pete.

"Nice shoes," he said.

I looked down at the glittering evening sandals. "Thanks," I said. "You know my cousin Angelo, who works in the morgue? His dad is a cobbler."

Pete looked puzzled.

I tried again. "A shoemaker—you know? He does custom work for the rich."

Pete shook his head. "Are you related to everyone in this town?"

"Not everyone." I smiled. A man in uniform was walking over to us. "No cops in the family."

Rick Spenser—Spense to his friends— strode to a halt in front of me. He frowned. I wasn't a friend, but we had gone to school together, so Spense knew all about my connections. Hence the frown.

"Well, well. Gina Gallo, what a surprise. The girl with the longest confession."

I choked. Beside me, Pete strangled a laugh.

"Don't see you in church much these days."

"The nuns frighten me." I worked to make my voice sound smooth.

Spense stared a hole through me, as if trying to figure out if I was serious or not.

"You know the vic?"

I nodded. "He's Tony Rizzo, a cousin-in-law by marriage, from New York."

At Saint Bonaventure Secondary, Spense had been tall, thin and nerdy. Now, he looked even taller, thinner and baffled. "What the hell is a cousin-in-law by marriage?"

"My cousin Marco—you remember Marco from high school with the souped-up Camaro?"

Spense nodded. In the old days, he had loved cars.

"Well, Marco moved to New York and married Tina Rizzo. Tony is her brother."

"So he's your cousin's wife's brother."

Spense shook his head. "You people are loaded with relatives."

I just shrugged.

"What was he doing in Hamilton?"

"Not sure," I said carefully. "Visiting family. I think he was interested in collecting art. You'll have to ask my uncle about that."

I heard Pete snort beside me. The only art this guy collected would have come from gas stations and porn shops.

"Are you in the art biz now?" Spense asked.

"No, no." I shook my head. "I'm a gemologist."

Spense raised an eyebrow. "Certified and everything?"

I nodded. "Got my degree first. Geology and chemistry."

Spense seemed impressed. "You always were smart." His eyes shifted to my décolletage and lingered there too long.

Pete was looking at me, curious. I could feel his attention as surely as if his arm had been wrapped around my shoulders. His eyes flipped back to Spense, and he frowned.

Spense shifted his gaze. "Malone, you got anything to do with this?"

Pete leaned back in the chair and folded his arms. His solid body overflowed the leather back.

"Just working my beat. And making sure you don't harass the witnesses."

"You got a lot of nerve, paperboy. I oughta thump you one."

"You can try."

That seemed to get Spense nicely upset. "That's it. Goddamn reporters. Down to the station, both of you."

Pete stood up and winked at me. This was his way of ensuring I didn't have to face the music alone. I could learn to appreciate a man like that.

We took Pete's sweet little convertible rather than ride in the cop car. I tried to hold my long hair down with one hand, but it was going to look like '80s big hair after the ride, no matter what.

We got to the station in under five minutes. As it happened, Spense didn't keep us long. They took us to separate poky little rooms that also had gray walls but no art. They grilled us about what we saw, what we heard, who else was there. They asked all sorts of personal stuff that probably wasn't strictly allowed, but I saw no reason to hide. I'll buy that Spense might need my phone number for follow-up, but was it really necessary to determine that I lived alone?

We must have given the same answers to the important questions, because they let us go half an hour later. Pete dropped me off at my small condo. I had to stop myself from inviting him upstairs.

"So…" he drawled as he opened the car door for me. "About that never calling before. You free tomorrow night?"

I hesitated. "I don't think I can do tomorrow. But what about the night after?"

Pete beamed. "Done. I know a nice place on James. Called La Paloma."

It was my turn to grin. "It's good," I said. "My cousin Vito owns it."

Pete rolled his eyes.

"Falling for the Goddaughter. I must be nuts." He laughed as he got back in the car. "Oh, and wear those shoes. I've got a thing for shoes."

"So do I," I said softly. "You have no idea."

I watched him drive off and wondered if it could be workable.

CHAPTER THREE

Around nine the next night, I waited in a coffee shop, nursing a double cream, no sugar. Angelo came to the door, looked around and spotted me. He smiled in a crooked way and made his way over. The black bag he carried matched mine. He slung it to the floor.

"All in there, Gina. I'll take your bag when I go. Dad says hi, by the way, and when are you going to come over for that shoe fitting. Red leather, with a stacked heel, just like you ordered."

"I'll be over soon. Did you have any trouble?"

Angelo grinned. "Nada. Place is so quiet—"

"—it's like a morgue. I know. That's getting old, sweetie."

He sat back. "No worries anyway. I'll manage the switch."

I nodded toward the coffee counter. "You want anything?"

Angelo shook his head. He had thick curls like the kind you see on those chubby angel drawings that seem to be everywhere. "Nah. Can't sleep if I have caffeine at night. Besides, I'm just on a break. Gotta get back to the morgue."

I took a sip of coffee.

"You know why he got hit?"

Angelo frowned and leaned forward. "Heard he slashed a hooker. I think he got too dangerous to keep around, and the

New York people wanted him done out of the city. It wasn't us."

I was thoughtful. That's what Uncle Vince had told me this morning. *It wasn't us.* Perhaps he knew I needed to hear it from someone else. Or perhaps it was even true.

"Come around to this side and give me a hug," I said. "Then you can pick up my bag."

Angelo got up and did that.

"Give my love to Aunt Vera," I whispered.

"Done," he said, and was gone.

I waited two minutes to finish the coffee, picked up Angelo's bag and went home.

In the privacy of my study, I took the dead guy's shoes out of the bag. Angelo would be taking a nearly identical pair back to the morgue.

I placed the shoes on the worktable. A special screwdriver helped me to disconnect the heel of one shoe from the body. The cavity was packed with stuffing to keep the contents from rattling. I carefully removed everything and counted.

Seven gemstones lay on the tabletop. Two were over two carats, and one was a beaut. A stunning pear-shaped sapphire, at least ten carats in weight. I looked through my loupe to see that it didn't disappoint—no visible inclusions.

They might strip-search you when coming through customs, but they don't usually take apart your shoes.

Which is a good thing, because we have a thing for shoes in our family.

CHAPTER FOUR

S ammy the String Bean phoned at dawn. Sammy is Vince's Jewish cousin and skinny sidekick. Yes, we can buy both our salami and mortadella wholesale in this family.

"We got a problem," he said.

I groaned. I hate it when they say "we," especially—dammit—before seven in the morning.

"Those rocks? They weren't supposed to come to us."

"You gotta be kidding." I was sitting up in bed now, wide awake.

"Vinnie says so. The Battalias in Buffalo? They were the pickup. 'Cept they didn't."

"Why the hell not?"

Okay, I was miffed now. At least three hundred g's of hot rocks on my hands, and they weren't even mine. Well, of course they weren't mine...I mean, I wasn't supposed to have them. They weren't mine *and* I wasn't supposed to have them.

"Joey—the Battalias' pickup stooge—went AWOL. Got crazy with a dame he met in a bar in North Tonawanda—where do they get these names? Anyway, Joey didn't show, so Tony just carried on with the next part of the assignment, which was to meet with us. So the shoes came over the border with him."

I took a breath.

"He didn't know what was in the shoe? Why?"

"'Cause they don't—didn't—trust the knob with knowing things like that. Not a rocket scientist. They just tell him to wear the shoes, and go visit whoever."

"Whomever," I said automatically. I didn't bother to correct the tense.

"You got it." Sammy agreed. "And we weren't the who." He snickered. It sounded like a donkey with laryngitis. "Hey, The Who—get it? We're not The Who."

Sammy is an acquired taste.

I was out of bed now, looking out the window. Bright sunshine filtered through the smog. I could see smoke plumes rising from the steel plants off in the distance. Hamilton does it best.

"So what does Vince want me to do?" I asked.

"Go to Buffalo. We're making the link with the Battalias now."

"Drive or fly?"

"Drive. You know—go shopping or something. Women stuff. Border cops believe that crap."

"Bugger," I muttered. This was not part of my plan for the day. Actually, it wasn't part of the plan for my life. I decided to remind Sammy.

"Nope," I said.

"Huh?"

"Not doing it," I said firmly. "This wasn't part of the deal, remember? I came back to run the jewelry store and do appraisals when called upon. That was the deal. Not running courier, or playing Mata Hari, or anything else to do with the other business interests you and Vince have. I'm through with that. It's why I left in the first place."

There was silence. I could hear the hum of the refrigerator two rooms away.

"Sammy?"

"I heard you. I remember."

He ought to. I'd only been back for a year. And it took them two months to find me, and another seven to sweet-talk me back.

More silence. A whole lot more, in fact. I'm not good at silence. So I said, "I don't owe you anything. You got what you wanted. I came back. I'm looking after the store. Clients respect me."

More silence. I can't abide silence. "Did you hear me, Sammy?"

"Yeah. Gotta go." He hung up.

I stared at the wall for a moment, holding my breath. Then I let out the air with a whoosh. Well, that's that, then. I was feeling pretty proud of myself. First time I ever said no to them. This was a historic day. Damn, I was hot.

Then why was I so uneasy?

The phone rang in my hand. I looked down. Different number.

I put it down on the bed. Paced the room. Waited until all eight rings were done (exactly eight—Uncle Vince always counts).

No more. I wasn't going to be pushed around anymore. I marched to the bathroom, grabbed a hairbrush and started massacring my hair. I yanked the brush through the unruly curls until they got caught. Then I yanked some more.

They knew the rules. They knew I wasn't playing the game—not *that* game, or any game! And unless it was something really important, life-threatening, in fact—

I ran back to the bed and picked up the phone. I called my cousin Paulo, the lawyer. He was a smart guy. He'd be in the know.

"What's the deal with Sammy and the rocks? How serious is this?" I asked.

Paulo sighed. "Don't involve me in this, okay? I got too much involvement already."

"Fine by me." I hung up. Paulo always was a wiener. I don't know why I bothered to call him.

I moved to the walk-in closet and started whipping out clothes. Sapphire-blue skirt and matching jacket with cute little tie belt in front. *He's* got too much involvement.

I've had involvement up the ying-yang for years and years. Where was that white tank top? Involvement was the whole reason I got out of this burg in the first place. Who needs family like mine?

Twenty minutes in the bathroom got me put together and presentable. All I had to do was get out of the condo—

The phone rang again. I let it go to the answering machine.

"Gina? It's your auntie. Sammy just told me."

Oh frig. It was Aunt Miriam—Sammy's wife. They brought in the big guns. I picked up the phone.

"It's just a little trip, maideleh—can't imagine why you wouldn't want to do a teeny-weeny thing like that as a favor to your dear uncle who loves you so—"

I missed the rest because the door was being pounded out of the wall.

"Hold on," I said into the phone.

I marched to the door and peered through the peephole.

Angelo stood there with two coffees and chagrin on his face.

I whooshed the door open.

"They sent you too?"

He nodded. "I'm supposed to say 'please.' And Luca's on his way over with cannoli."

Aunt Miriam was still squawking into the phone. Before I could put it to my ear, the cell phone in my purse starting singing "Shut Up and Drive."

"That's probably Uncle Vito," Angelo said.

"For Christ's sake! It's the full onslaught from all sides." I threw up my arms. "You know what that means. This could go on for days."

He shrugged. "Can you sort of speed things up a bit and say yes? I've got a lot going on right now."

I whammed the door all the way open. It bounced off the back wall. "Might as well come in. One of those better have cream in it."

I put the phone to my ear again.

"Aunt Miriam?"

"Gone to the can. She handed it back to me."

"Sammy?" I sighed. "How desperate is he?"

"It's the border crossing. Doesn't trust anyone else to get through it without messing up. Think of it this way. The rocks don't belong here. You're taking them back to where they kinda legally belong."

Yeah, right. As if the city of Buffalo were the rightful owner. I looked down at the floor. It didn't look back.

"Just this once, right? And you owe me!"

"Of course, doll. You call the shots."

Yeah, and I'm Pamela Anderson's twin sister.

"All right. You want me to meet up with this Joey, right? The little skirt-chaser."

"Not so little," Sammy said. "Joey is over three hundred. Used to play football for the Ti-Cats."

"Oh, *that* Joey!" Missing a few brain cells after all those concussions, poor boy. "I've met him. Aunt Vera tried to set me up with him once."

He laughed. "Joey with the precious goddaughter? Bet that went down great with Vinnie."

"Like shoes on a goat."

I hung up, took the coffee from Angelo and started looking for my passport.

CHAPTER FIVE

My car is pretty nondescript. I'd love a hot little convertible like Pete's, but when you carry a lot of—shall we say *expensive*—merchandise, as a rule you opt for safe and staid. Doesn't tempt the joyriders.

I stopped for gas at my cousin Guytano's station. Some high-school kid was working the pumps, so I didn't stick around to say hi. Then I hit Main to stop at a bank machine. I saw an empty parking space across the street and made for it. Main is one way, and it is much easier to dash a block down to King than to turn left, and then left again, trying to find a space. Hard to explain, but if you live in a city of one-way streets, you'll get it.

I grabbed my handbag-cum-suitcase and bolted through the traffic.

Only one person in front of me at the ATM—I was in luck.

Two minutes later, I turned away from the bank machine and bashed right into Pete Malone.

"Jeez, you scared me," I said, trying to catch my breath.

"I'm not so scary," Pete quipped. One hand reached out to steady me. A spark shot through me at his touch.

"What are you *doing* here?" I blurt out. Was he following me? Normally, I wouldn't mind, but this was damned inconvenient at the moment.

"I was getting coffee next door. Saw you rush up." He looked amused.

"Oh. Well, nice to see you. Pete, I'd love to stay and chat, but I'm in a big hurry. Call me, okay?" I turned abruptly, nearly tripping on the cracked pavement.

Pete was right beside me as I hoofed it, or tried to hoof it, back to my car. These shoes were four inches of stacked-heel torture.

"Wait a minute! We're having dinner tonight, remember?"

I stopped and turned. "Oh crap, Pete! I am so sorry. Of course we are. It's not that I forgot—it's just—"

BAM!

"What the hell was *that*?"

The whole ground seem to shake for a moment, and then someone screamed.

Pete grabbed my arm. Sirens blasted all over the place. Police cars came screeching—all of them, I swear—the entire Steeltown contingent. They careened up the street and slammed to a stop in front of the bank across the street.

"Run!" I yelled. What can I say? It's instinctive.

Pete just held me tighter.

"The big bad policemen won't get you. Promise."

We stood across the street and watched the action at the other bank. Car doors slammed, and there was a lot of yelling. I tried to keep out of sight and peered out from behind Pete's shoulder. Man, he smelled good—like bread just out of the oven. Yum.

"Looks like a robbery."

"Yup," I said, watching more cops pile out and pull guns.

"Anyone you know?" Pete asked innocently.

I would have whacked him, but he had my arms pinned.

"Got to be first-timers, blowing a safe like that. No one blows up safes anymore."

Pete raised an eyebrow.

"The trick is to get in and out fast," I said in disgust. "You can't blow up things and do that."

We stared at the lockdown from the alley between two buildings across the street.

"Well, that's just perfect," I muttered. "What the hell am I going to do now?"

"Explain?"

"My car's over there, behind the wall of cops." Think hard, Gina. Okay, I had everything I needed. Passport in pocket. I was wearing my new shoes with the custom compartments. I had a pair of ballerina flats in my handbag to change into after the drop. So I had everything to make the Buffalo contact, except the vehicle to get me there.

I could rent a car, maybe. Or I could take a plane. Probably quicker to drive, but a rental car might be trouble at the border. Okay, it's a plane and then a taxi from the airport.

"Pete, can you drive me to the airport?"

He frowned and released me. "Where the hell were you going today?"

Oh right. I was supposed to meet him for dinner tonight. Backpedal.

"Just to Buffalo. I was going to drive and be back in time for dinner, but I don't want to bother renting a car. Important meeting," I said. I even nodded. That should make it look authentic.

"Ah." Pete looked relieved. "We can go together. We'll take my car."

Crap.

"Oh now, I couldn't." It was true. I couldn't. I also couldn't tell him why I couldn't.

"Nonsense, no trouble at all. It's only an hour away. I've got my Nexus card on me. I can stop at WBEN Radio while we're there. We can even have dinner over the border. I know this little place in Amherst."

I fiddled with the handles of my handbag. "Don't you have to go to work?"

He laughed. "It's Friday. They owe me about a month of overtime. Besides, I'm working on a story about cross-border rivalries between football teams and can talk to the guys at WBEN about it. I'll drop you off where you have to be and then come back and pick you up. Then we do dinner."

This could work, I thought. Maybe it would even be a good cover.

"Where do you need to go?"

"The Walden Galleria shopping center." I said it without thinking.

He looked straight at me. "For a business meeting?"

I gulped again. "They have offices above the stores." Didn't they?

He tilted his head and shrugged. "Let's go, then. I'm parked over here."

CHAPTER SIX

Buffalo used to be a booming dynamic city in the 1800s. You can still see vestiges of the grand old gal as you drive through areas such as Amherst. But for me, the glory of Buffalo will always be the Martin House, designed by Frank Lloyd Wright in his early days. It's under reconstruction now, or I would have insisted on Pete taking a detour.

Hamilton is only an hour from Buffalo, but you need a passport or Nexus card to get into the United States from Canada now. In the old days, we used to hop across the border for dinner on the other side with a mere flip of a driver's license. Usually, customs officials didn't even ask to see it. Most of the time, they'd ask us what the specials were tonight at John's Flaming Hearth, and maybe join us at the bar after they got off shift.

The world was different now. I was expecting the worst, but going through customs was just one more surprise in a day of surprises. Pete drove up to one of the many kiosks at the Peace Bridge. The middle-aged redhead in the booth beamed a toothy smile.

"Hi, Pete," she said. "Staying for a while this time?"

Pete—the dirty dog—smiled back. "Nah, just a day trip. Taking the lady shopping at the Galleria."

Her smile changed to a frown. Reddy-locks peered in at me. "Where you from, Miss?"

"Hamilton," I replied, in my sunniest voice. "Born and bred."

"Passport."

I handed it to Pete, who duly presented it.

Back it came through the open window.

"Nice to see you, Marcie." Pete can be a charmer.

The smile was back on her face. "Have a nice time there."

I waited until we were clear of the exit before starting the interrogation.

"Who's the dye job?" I asked in my most nonchalant manner.

Pete glanced over. "Jealous?"

"No, I like my hair." Sometimes you gotta be obtuse.

Pete laughed. "I cross the border every other week. You get to know the people with the power."

I cocked my head. "Care to elaborate?"

"I was born here," Pete said simply. "My folks live here."

Well, that explains the Nexus card.

"They have a house in Amherst. Kind of old."

Figures.

"They also have a place in Florida."

Better.

We were on some highway now. At this speed, it was hard to hear. I kept my questions for later.

* * *

Half an hour later, I was sitting on a bench in the Galleria, massaging my right foot. I deliberately avoided the Macy's end so I wouldn't run into my drop contact ahead of time. Why? Pete had insisted on coming into the mall so we could agree on a spot to meet later. I had insisted on finding a bench so I could sit down and take off my shoes. They were killing me.

"Nice place," Pete said, gazing down the length of gilded stores. "Used to be classier, and a whole lot busier. Place is a morgue now during the day."

I looked up. "You know this mall?"

"I grew up not far from here," Pete said.

"So you know the people at WBEN."

Pete smiled. I felt my heart teeter.

"Did an internship there when I was in high school. You know, the work experience thing. Made a lot of great friends and contacts. Then they followed me when I was in the pros. Local boy makes good. Until I didn't." Pete looked off in the distance, thinking about those days, no doubt. I didn't want him to feel sad, so I rushed to speak.

"I'll bet you took a lot of girlfriends here." Why did I say that? Of all the stupid things…

Pete looked up in surprise. Then he raised an eyebrow. "Only one. I went with one girl all through school. I'm the monogamous sort."

I felt my face go red. What can you say to top that?

"So I'll meet you back here at five."

"Right," I said, looking up and away. "Opposite the lingerie store there." I shifted over on the bench to make room for a large-breasted blond woman. She smiled her thanks.

Pete wandered up to the window with his hands in his pockets. "Come look at this." He nodded to the strappy satin nightgown in the window. "You like that sort of thing?"

I grabbed the pair of flats from my handbag-cum-suitcase and put them on. Then I rushed to join him at the window.

"It's beautiful," I said. Just looking at it made my heart sing.

"You'd look good in pink. Although you look pretty good in that blue suit too," said Pete.

I felt a charge hit me clear through the chest. Damn, but he looked good from the side. Something about the casual way he stood with his hand in his pocket, the way his hair fell over his eyes, which were fixed on the mannequin...

I shook myself. "That's fuchsia. Guys never know colors."

"Red, blue, yellow and green. And orange. That's all I need to know."

"What about purple?"

"And purple."

"What about brown, gray and beige? Chartreuse? Puce?"

"Never heard of it. You're making that up, right?"

Men. I shook my head and turned back to the bench. The blond woman was gone. And so were my...

"Bloody hell!" I yelled. I dashed around the back of the bench. Nothing.

"What is it?" Pete was baffled.

"My shoes! My shoes are gone!"

I was scrambling now, knees on the floor, looking under everything in sight.

"When did you last see them?"

"I left them on the floor right here. Then you called me over to look at the window, and then"—I was starting to wail—"they aren't here!"

I stood up and scanned both right and then left. No sign of the blond woman. Where could she have gone in that time?

Maybe she dashed into a store? A change room? If I tried to search every change room in the place, someone would call security for sure...

"Ah." His voice relaxed. "Don't worry about that. I'll buy you another pair. I bet they have some really nice ones in—"

He stopped when he saw my face.

"It's not just the shoes, is it?"

I hesitated, then shook my head.

"Was something in the shoes?" His voice was tense.

I gulped.

His hand went to his forehead and brushed back hair nervously. "Don't tell me it's drugs," he hissed. "Don't tell me I just smuggled drugs over the border."

I shook my head. "Not drugs."

He let out a sigh. "I'm not going to like this, am I?"

"Not so much." It was hard to breathe. I flopped down on the bench.

"You going to tell me?"

I thought for maybe two seconds, then shook my head.

"Mind if I guess?"

I thought for maybe three seconds, then shook my head.

"Does it have anything to do with the business you're in?"

I didn't move.

"And maybe that store over there, the one with the flashy things in the window that people might buy for engagement gifts?"

I looked up at him.

"Okay." He plunked down on the bench beside me. "What do we do first?"

I think that's when I started to fall in love with Pete Malone.

CHAPTER SEVEN

We found the women's washroom. Luckily, it was empty. I took out my cell phone, punched numbers and waited for the "Hullo."

"Sammy, I lost the shoes." Have you ever tried to yell without raising your voice?

A pause.

"What do you mean, lost the shoes?"

I took a breath. "The shoes, Sammy! The shoes. I put them down on the floor by a bench and someone walked off with them."

"*Holy crap!*" He got it now. "You lost the fucking shoes! Why the hell did you take them off?"

This is where it got tricky. "They were making my feet hurt. I switched them after we got across the border and put on flats instead."

Another pause.

"Who's the *we*?"

A blast of cold hit my face. Crap. I blew it. Sammy may be rough, but he isn't stupid.

"We." I swallowed. Tried to breathe. "You know that bank robbery on King? My car was in the parking lot, and I decided to leave it there because I didn't want to be frisked—you know, scene of the crime, and me being who I am and what I was carrying—so I got someone to drive me here."

"Who *someone*?"

"Um…Pete Malone."

I heard real bad cursing. Real bad. Aunt Miriam would have his nuts for noodles if she knew.

"How much does he know?" Sammy said finally.

"Nothing. He thinks we're going out to dinner tonight after I do a little shopping." Lie, lie, lie. I'm going to hell, no question.

"Vinnie ain't gonna like this." I could almost hear him shaking his head.

"Vince doesn't have to know about it. At least not yet. Look, I need you to call the Battalia people and tell them there's been a slight delay. We'll make the trade tomorrow, same time. Can you do that?"

"You going to be able to get them back by tomorrow?"

"Sure." My voice swaggered with confidence. "I know exactly who took them. And that woman has no idea what's in them, so we're safe."

"She just wanted the shoes?"

"You got it. Now I just have to go after her and get them back."

We rang off. I left the washroom and found Pete leaning against a wall with his big arms crossed. He looked over and met my eyes.

"Any idea where to start?" he asked.

"Not a clue," I said.

CHAPTER EIGHT

The local food factory served large mugs of pretty good coffee. This was a good thing. I needed a whole lot of coffee to clear my brain. Or maybe I just needed a new brain.

We were seated at a table for two. As per my training, I had grabbed the chair that allowed me to look out across the restaurant, with my back to the wall. Like in the old westerns.

"I hate my life," I mumbled into the mug.

"Why don't you change it then?"

I looked up sharply. If Pete was trying to be helpful, he had a lot to learn.

"I did try." The look I gave him wasn't warm. "I left Hamilton two years ago to do my own thing in a place far away. They found me eventually and convinced me to come back. It took awhile." I took a slurp.

Now he looked serious. "That doesn't seem right."

"You don't understand." I shook my head firmly. "They brought me back for my own safety. Two attempts had already been made to kidnap me. I was a sitting target for anyone who had a thing against my Uncle Vince. Still am, in fact. But on his home turf, they don't dare try it. Besides, I like Hamilton. I wanted to come home."

I did too. Yeah, it was a bit smoggy, and some people would call it a backwater compared to Toronto. But it was right on the lake, and it was *real*, if you get what I mean. It wasn't pretending to be anything it wasn't.

No "World Class" about it, unless they've started a category for mid-century industrial. And it has character. Not to mention a pile of great Italian restaurants.

Pete was still frowning. "It's not fair that you have to live your life by their terms."

I sighed. "I don't, really. It's on my terms now. Except I shouldn't have agreed to do this little rendezvous. I capitulated in a weak moment. Believe me, I won't ever do it again." No kidding. I could hardly have bungled it more.

Pete sat back and seemed to relax a bit. "I can't imagine what your life has been like."

"I had a good childhood." I swirled the coffee around in the mug. Lovely aroma coming up. "Mom was a great mom. She's in Florida now with husband number two. He's a nice guy, a retired engineer. She met him a few years ago, when she stayed at a resort down there."

"What happened to husband number one?"

"Ah." I slurped again. "Now that's a puzzle. He kind of disappeared before I was born."

"What kind of 'disappeared'? He left town? Or something else?"

"Couldn't help you there. The story is he got scared, so he took off. Our family didn't have anything to do with it. They all seem pretty baffled about where the guy got to. And I know when they're lying."

Pete went silent for a moment. "So you grew up without a father?"

"Yes, but don't go feeling sorry for me. I had plenty of family around me growing up. Several aunts and uncles and exactly twenty-four cousins, to be exact." Oops. Too many *exacts* in that sentence. Maybe I needed some food. I hadn't had breakfast.

"You hungry?"

"I'm always hungry! I could eat a skunk."

He laughed. "Always, you say the one thing I'd never guess. Why a skunk?"

I shrugged. "Wouldn't want to eat a horse. I like them. Skunks, not so much."

"Not sure they have skunks on the menu here. They may have brunch though. I can personally vouch for the—"

"Holy cow, Pete—that's her!" I was out of my seat and pointing through the restaurant window.

"What?"

"Right over there, talking to that man. The blowsy blond with the huge—crikey! She's turning away and—she's going to leave the mall, Pete! I have to follow her."

"Hold on while I leave some cash—"

I grabbed my purse and pushed away from the table. "I'm going after her!"

I ran. Chairs fell, and a few people swore.

Behind me, someone was yelling my name.

CHAPTER NINE

Two hours later, my purse was singing "Shut up and Drive" again. I held my breath, then made a dive for the cell phone.

"Gina?"

"Um…hi, Sammy. I was just going to call you." I held the phone close against my mouth. "I may not be able to make that drop tomorrow."

Silence. "Where the hell are ya?"

"It's not that I don't know where the shoes are. I can actually see them from here. It's just that I gotta find a way to get them off the goddamn thief who's wearing them, without causing a riot."

Another pause. "Where are you?" Sammy said again.

I tried to sound casual. "In a restaurant." A restaurant in a very big airport, but he didn't have to know that. And I wasn't exactly *in* the restaurant, but I could see it from here. I tried to shut out the noise of the planes with my hand.

"In Buffalo?"

"Er…not exactly."

"Where, *exactly*?"

"Would you believe…Toronto?" I hoped he wouldn't.

"You're kidding me. You're back in Canada?"

"She got in a car and drove to Toronto! I couldn't tackle her in public—there were two police cars in the parking lot on a coffee break. I could see the cops gabbing through open windows. Blondie would have screamed the house down if I tried something. What was I to do? She was wearing the bloody shoes, and I had to go after them." It was obvious. Why couldn't he see that?

"Paperboy still with you?"

Now I gulped. "Um...yeah, actually."

Sammy swore. "And he don't know anything about this, right?"

I was silent.

"Sugar, you're gonna have to marry the dude, or we're going to have to whack him. You've got twenty-four hours."

I clicked the Off button. We were in the lineup for the airline counter. I looked over at Pete, who smiled back at me. A nice innocent smile. What a nice guy. Given the choice, I hoped Pete was a commitment kind of man. For his sake.

"You didn't tell him we were at the airport," Pete said. He raised one eyebrow.

I squirmed a bit. "Why alarm the poor man? He has enough to worry about."

Besides, I had no idea where we were going.

Luckily, Pete had an answer for that.

"Her luggage tag is for Phoenix. How do you feel about making a trip to the desert?"

I took a deep breath and released it slowly. Good thing I had the company credit card on me. We moved to the head of the line. Then we were signaled over to the ticket counter.

I slapped my plastic down and asked for two seats to Phoenix.

"Just a minute—" said Pete, reaching for his wallet.

"Not now," I whispered back.

The clerk was a little brunette whose big brown eyes had latched on to Pete. He smiled back.

"The flight is almost full. I can get you on it, but not two seats together. One in row fifteen. One in row twenty-three."

"Nothing together?"

"Sorry, ma'am."

Ma'am? Since when had I become my mother? I sighed.

"We'll take them." Four hours to Arizona sitting beside someone I didn't know, or worse, some guy with garlic on his breath. I was gonna hate it.

"Do you have luggage to check?" the clerk asked.

"Just carry-on."

Ticket lady handed Pete the tickets and the boarding passes. Never mind that I had paid for them.

As we walked away, Pete said, "Look, I didn't mean for you to pay for my ticket. Let me—"

I waved dismissively. "We're supposed to be traveling together. It's all part of the cover."

He murmured something about paying me back later. That had me wondering. Did he mean the money? Or was this some other form of "payback"?

Next stop was airport security.

I'm always nervous going through security. Call it a professional hazard. I told myself that I wasn't carrying anything this time, so what's to worry? My passport was clean. So what if it wasn't my real name... the initials were the same. Gloria Grant. Easy to remember.

Guess Pete never noticed.

Pete sailed through pre-clearance with no problem. Smiles all around. I didn't even register a glance. So far, so good.

"Gate's this way," Pete said. "Want to grab a book or magazine?"

"Do they sell drugs?"

He smiled again. "No drugs, but a good book will pass the time."

He ushered me toward one of those sell-everything stores. I grabbed a bag of nuts and two candy bars. A book cover caught my eye. *Rowena Through the Wall*. I didn't know the author, but the cover was cool.

A couple were locked in a passionate embrace. I flipped it over.

"It's one of those time-travel stories. Might be fun," I said.

"Did you pose for the cover?"

I elbowed him in the side but had to admit the heroine did resemble me. Pete grabbed a couple of sports mags. He snatched the book and goodies out of my hand and went to pay.

As we walked to the gate, we heard loud male voices. At the entrance to the waiting area, I stopped with eyes wide and shuddered. I closed my eyes, then opened them again, hoping things would be different.

It was still all there. A group of older men in sports jerseys had obviously started happy hour early. On the other side were enough nuns for a choir. And not one but two crying babies. Pete led me to a pair of empty seats. At least we would be together until they called the flight.

One of the would-be jocks saw Pete and came over.

"Hey, you're that guy. The sportswriter guy." He turned back to the group before Pete could answer. "Hey, Larry. It's that sportswriter guy."

Larry came over, preceded by a huge beer gut. I don't think his knuckles were dragging on the ground, but it was close.

"Aren't you—?" Larry scratched his head in deep thought.

"I told you, he's the sportswriter guy." Another inebriated chubby bloke ambled up.

"Pete Malone," Pete offered. He was smiling widely.

"Naw, that's not it."

I choked on air.

"Hey, Bob, what's this guy's name? You remember."

"Dick? Dick something."

"That's it!"

Pete shook his head. He wasn't smiling now. Pete was a newspaper guy. It wasn't nice to be mistaken for another sports reporter on some local TV station.

I, however, was having a great time.

"Sure it is. Watch you all time. How about those Leafs, eh?" He socked Pete/Dick in the shoulder. "Wait till I tell the guys back at the club. I met Dick What's-his-name."

"Nice ta meet ya, Dick."

The two ambled back to their group.

"I may have to kill someone," Pete said. He was gritting his teeth.

"Let me introduce you to my family," I said back.

CHAPTER TEN

The cell phone in my purse was singing again. I ignored it. It rang exactly eight times. I reached in to turn it off. For once in my life, they couldn't reach me. It felt good.

"Is she still there behind me?" Pete asked.

"Yup." I spotted Blondie as soon as we came to the waiting area. So had the jocks. Blondie seemed to be enjoying some attention. A short skirt and low-cut clingy top will do that. Several of the sports-jersey guys were leering. The Pete/Dick contingent were not too far gone on booze to miss Blondie's obvious attractions. Both of them.

And if those were natural, I was the Queen of Sheba.

"This is the first boarding call for flight 640 to Phoenix, Arizona. Would people needing assistance and parents traveling with small children murph murph murph..." The words faded into general noise. I looked around for Blondie and saw her get up.

Pete squeezed my hand. Moments later, it was time for the rest of us to board. We filed onto the plane. I took the seat in row fifteen, and Pete went farther down.

I felt lonely. This wasn't good. I shouldn't be growing so attached to this guy. It was dangerous in just so many ways. For one thing, I had a job to do on this trip. For another, there was the family... You never could tell how they would react to an outsider.

I put my carry-on up in the overhead bin and prepared to sit. A man in a T-shirt and tattoos tapped me on the arm.

"Your husband." He jerked his thumb over his shoulder. "Asked me to trade seats with you."

"My husband did that." I looked down the aisle. Pete waved. I smiled back. "Thank you. Thank you very much."

The tattoo man nodded. I got up, and he looked me over.

"Lucky man."

"He certainly is."

Pete moved over to the middle seat to give me the aisle. The fellow by the window seat was working on a BlackBerry.

"I didn't know we were married," I said. "Chivalry is not dead."

"Not dead, but the price has gone up."

"Hmmm?"

"Wasn't enough to make us married. I had to lay a hundred on him to get him to move."

Now I grinned. "I'm worth it," I said brightly. I reached for the seatbelt.

Pete leaned back and looked me up and down as if trying to decide. I slapped his arm.

"Since we are married, the proper response is 'Yes, dear.'"

Pete laughed out loud. "Yes, dear."

The babies had settled down to whimpers. The jocks were asking when the bar opened. The nuns were praying. What the heck. I offered up a Hail Mary myself just as the plane started to back away from the gate. Pete took my hand.

I don't mind airplanes. But it kind of felt nice to have my hand held, so I didn't say anything.

Once in the air, Pete poked me to get my attention.

"So...we got on the plane. We're following Blondie to God's country. A little unexpected for a weekday. Not that I mind going on an adventure. But I gotta ask, do we actually have a plan for getting back the shoes?"

I shrugged. "It's complicated. But here's what I've been thinking."

And I told him.

He stared at me, eyes wide, and shook his head. Not a good sign. Then he threw back his head and laughed.

"Okay, can you think of a better plan?" I was a little miffed.

"Oh, no. This is your event. You get to do the master planning. I'm just along for the ride. And to pay for dinner."

"Right!" I said happily. "I remember. This is our dinner date. I get real food. I love real food. I am so not a salad girl."

He chuckled and shook his head.

"What?" I glared at him. "You don't think I look undernourished?"

Those wonderful hazel eyes twinkled. "You look great. You look perfect. I mean that. You have one hell of a figure."

I could feel myself blush. My face was searing hot. There was only one way to answer this.

"Why, thank you!" I said. "I work hard to keep each part well fed."

Now he roared. His laughing woke the baby two rows over, and it started wailing. Then the other baby joined in.

The guys in the sports jerseys were getting louder.

I ignored them all. A girl has to keep her composure.

After the free coffee and soda pop came (beer and wine extra), Pete decided to watch a movie. We shared the snacks, and I settled into my book.

At the end of the movie, the cart came around with the stale sandwiches. Pete asked for a pop.

"Want anything?" he asked me.

I shook my head. "I can wait until Phoenix. Then I want a real meal. Steak and a baked potato, with sour cream *and* butter. Fried mushrooms. A side of asparagus. And cheesecake." Oh yeah. I was ready for a pig-out.

Pete grinned. He shook his head. "Always, you surprise me. How's the book?" He took a swig of pop.

"Great! Really funny," I said. "I like the sex."

He choked on the pop.

The captain came on the PA system and told us about the altitude we were flying at (33,000 feet), when we would get to Phoenix (at 4:05 their time) what the weather would be like when we got there (hot), and things we could do once we got there.

He had a nice voice.

"When you're in Phoenix, be sure to visit the Arizona Biltmore Hotel, which was designed in the 1930s by Frank Lloyd Wright and his students. I've stayed there and can personally recommend both restaurants."

Restaurants! Yum. I was hungry.

There was a pause. Then a female voice came over the PA, fainter but more strident. *"You never took me to the Biltmore. Oh no, I'm only good enough for Motel 5!"*

"Shut up, Charlene. You never complained at the time."

"At the time, I didn't know you were married!" said the female voice.

"Sure you didn't."

Pete looked at me. His eyes went wide. "They forgot to turn off the mic," he said.

The cabin went quiet. The drunken guys stopped hollering. Absolutely everyone was focused on the drama beyond the cockpit door.

"I'll bet you take your wife to the Biltmore. I bet you've stayed there lots of times with her."

"Charlene, I told you. We don't have sex anymore."

"You don't have sex with me anymore either! Who's the new one, Frank? Who is she?

That slag from United? The one with the fake boobs?"

"Stop whacking me! Cut that out. Godamnit, I'm the captain!"

The silence in the cabin turned to chortles and gasps. Someone started to choke. Pete was doing that silent laughter thing while his whole face went red.

"Mother was right!" Sob! *"Never date a pilot. Why didn't I listen?"*

The cockpit door flung open, and a distraught flight attendant lurched down the aisle. She was pretty in an Anne Hathaway kind of way and would have been quite attractive if she hadn't been sniffling and muttering.

With a start, she seemed to realize where she was. She straightened. Her hand went to smooth down her skirt, and her face set to a professional smile.

She paused two rows ahead of us. Then a glint came to her eye. Her hand reached for a can of pop on someone's tray. She turned, went back through the door to the cockpit and raised the pop can.

I was at just the right angle to see her dump it all over his head.

"What the fuck?" the captain yelled.

Then she marched back through the cabin, turned and plunked her butt down in the empty aisle seat in front of us.

The middle-aged woman in the next seat patted her on the arm. "There, there, dear," she said. "Men are beasts, I tell you. Beasts! I should know—I married six of them."

Pete was close to expiring now. Tears were rolling down his face, and he was wheezing badly. I was really starting to worry.

"Christ," he said, "what more can happen now?"

CLUNK.

BANG.

WHOOSH.

"What the hell was *that*?" Pete yelled.

There was another *clunk* from the underbelly of the plane, and more screams. Then the plane started to dive.

"Holy mother of god!" Pete grabbed for me.

Lights flashed. The oxygen masks came down. More screaming.

"Put this on." He reached for one and shoved it on my face. "Don't argue!"

I wasn't arguing. I was all for oxygen at a time like this.

Lights went out completely. One flight attendant fell flat on the floor. Miss Motel 5 was lurching around the aisle holding on to seat backs.

"Frank, if you kill us, so help me God, I will cut your heart out!" she howled.

"Kind of redundant," Pete muttered through his mask. He held me as close as a person could be held.

One of the nuns started singing "Ave Maria." A few of the drunken sports-jersey guys joined in. I hoped God wasn't listening. It wouldn't help our chances.

The plane leveled off, and the lights came on.

"Just a spot of turbulence," came the voice over the PA system. It sounded reassuring. *"Sorry about that, people. All flight attendants to the cockpit, please."*

"I'll cockpit your cock!" yelled Miss Motel 5.

Pete relaxed his grip, then stared at me.

"Do you ever have a normal day?"

CHAPTER ELEVEN

I called home as soon as we landed.

"Sammy. You have no idea how good it is to hear your voice."

"Frig—Gina? Where the hell are you? Vinnie's having a crap. You're not in Toronto. We checked."

I didn't ask how they checked. They have ways.

"Arizona. Phoenix. Nice place. Hot. You'd like it."

More cursing.

"The shoes?"

"They're here."

"Okay, I'm sending someone down. She might need a little convincing."

"Sammy, no! You are not going to hurt the woman."

"Sugar! Relax. I just want the shoes. I'll bring another pair for trade. That's fair, right? See—nothing to worry about."

"Give me another day, Sammy! I got a plan. A cunning plan. Let me try it out."

There was a pause on the other end.

"One day, Sugar," Sammy said. "You got one day. Then me and Luca gets on a plane."

I clicked the phone shut and turned to Pete.

"We have exactly twenty-four hours to get those shoes back, or we move to Argentina. I hear it's nice there in winter."

CHAPTER TWELVE

It was a really swank hotel, I'll give her that. The place had a bunch of Egyptian-looking pillars out front and a pile of lighted fountains.

Phoenix was a classy place, if you stopped to look. Too bad we'd spent most of the last several hours following the silicon blond across the continent and hiding behind things. Not to mention piling a whack of airfares and other expenses on the company credit card.

At least now I had a plan. Sort of.

I walked in the front doors of the place and looked up. The lobby was completely open to the ceiling, which must have been fifteen stories high.

"Wow," I said. "This is huge! This is perfect."

"Sort of over the top, in my opinion," Pete said. He clearly wasn't keen on gold-covered plaster statues and ornate fountains.

"No, I mean the layout. All the rooms face onto this huge atrium. The corridors are open to the lobby all the way up. We'll be able to see what room she goes to without having to tail her."

Pete raised an eyebrow. "And then what?"

I scanned the huge reception area. There she was, at the counter.

"Easy-peasy. I've got a cunning plan." I did now too. What a relief.

Blondie turned away from the counter and started toward the gold-and-glass elevators.

Even better—we'd be able to see right into the elevator.

"We make out what floor she gets out on, then watch to see where she goes."

"Now I get it," Pete said. "We count over the number of doors from the corner."

"You got it!"

We watched in silence for a short while. Then I nudged him with my elbow. "There she goes. She's getting out on…one, two, three—the third floor."

She turned left coming out of the elevator and moved down the corridor. No way she'd notice us standing way down below in the lobby. Her whole focus was on finding the right room number.

She stopped. There was a pause as she fiddled with the swipe card. Then the door opened, and she disappeared from sight.

"Fourth from the end," Pete said.

"Hold on a minute. I'm going to check things out. Just wait here."

I made for the elevator, leaving a baffled Pete behind.

I got out on the third floor and went to the fourth room from the end. It said 323 on the door. Then I went back to the elevator and rode it down to join Pete.

"We want room 322," I said when we met up.

He raised an eyebrow. "And then what?"

"Trust me." I grabbed his arm. "All will be revealed. But I'm thinking it might be better if you get the room. Say I have a sentimental reason for wanting that room. And if they don't have 322 available, ask for 324." Room 324 was a long shot, but it was worth a try.

I watched as Pete sauntered up to the reception desk. A sweet-looking brunette gave him a big smile. I sighed.

While I waited, I looked around the lobby. Lots of businessmen were sitting in leather lounge chairs clicking away at their smartphones. Behind them were several trees in huge planters. A bar stood off in the distance. It had several customers.

Pete walked back to me. He was smiling.

"We got 322. It's your lucky day."

* * *

The room was straight out of a designer magazine. Shades of cream and mocha, with a king-size bed. Gorgeous, but I was a girl on a mission.

"Ha! I was right. Sometimes I am just so smart, I stun myself."

Pete looked puzzled again.

I pointed. "The connecting door—see? It leads to her room."

Now he frowned. Little furrows creased his forehead.

"Hotels all use swipe cards now," I explained. "How can you pick a lock with a swipe card? But then I reasoned that most of these rooms have connecting doors on one side for families. You can book two rooms and put your kids in the other."

Pete looked at me inquiringly. "How did you know which side the room with the connecting door would be on?"

"Now that's the really clever part. I figured they would go in pairs. So room one would connect with room two, three with four…"

"I get it—322 with 323." Pete smiled. "So we open the door on our side and…then what?

I twinkled at him.

"Wait and see."

* * *

Pete took me to dinner at a swank place close by called the Twisted Fork. I had everything I wanted—steak, baked potato, cheesecake and enough merlot to float a boat. Pete had the same. It was heaven. Nice to know we were food-compatible.

I dated a vegetarian once. That lasted until dinner the same day.

While Pete paid the bill, I played with my smartphone to find an address. We made a quick trip to a specialty store called Halloween City. We got back to the hotel around seven thirty. I tried on the maid costume we'd just purchased.

"It's a little skimpy," I said, pulling down the fifteen-inch skirt.

"I like it!" Pete was grinning.

"Yeah, but I don't think real maids wear this sort of thing."

"So...who's going to object?"

I scowled at him. Men.

"They'll think I'm a maid-for-hire, if you know what I mean."

Pete shrugged. "I'll be right there, in case of trouble."

Trouble. Like that's something I'm not acquainted with.

"You're just after a pair of shoes," he said. "It's not like we're robbing a bank or something. What could go wrong?"

I glanced over at him. "You don't know me very well yet, do you?"

He watched me take a specialty pick from my purse.

"Do I want to know what that is?" Pete asked. "Or where you got it?"

"I'm a gemologist. I have all sorts of tools, you know?"

"Do gemologists often have to pick locks?"

I opened the door on our end and listened.

All quiet inside. Out for dinner, for sure. Hopefully, she wasn't wearing the shoes. Hopefully, they would be in the room, all by their little selves. I worked my little tool—lovely thing—and carefully pushed the door wide open.

"What the hell?" A balding older man with a potbelly and no clothes lurched off the bed.

"Oops," I said.

"Who the hell are you?" The blond with the Dolly Parton hair was also wearing no clothes.

In situations like this, I find it best to say nothing. Besides, Blondie was starting to look emotional. I don't think her face was normally that color.

"Oh, I get it! Busting in on my turf, are you? Who sent you? Marty? Did Marty send you? I'll have his balls for earrings, I will." Blondie pushed off the far side of the bed with both hands to land on her feet. Then she poked a finger through the air at me. "And I got to tell you, ho, that maid getup is just too old."

"I like it," the fat man said. He reached for a pillow to cover his wobbly bits.

"Harry, you'd like a knothole in a pine tree."

"Are we doing a threesome?" Now he sounded excited.

"I'm not doing no threesome. Nobody told me about this, so just get out of here, little miss bouncy maid and find your own john."

Little miss bouncy maid?

Blondie waved her arms around. "So you look a little like Catherine Zeta-Jones—is that who they're trying to pass you off as? Well, I've been in the look-alike business a lot longer than you, and believe me, sister, you're just a baby."

So that's what was up with the Dolly Parton hair. She was supposed to be a Dolly look-alike!

One thing I could tell for sure. She wasn't a natural blond.

From the connecting doorway, someone sniggered. I had a good idea who it might be.

So I wasn't surprised when he peeked his head around the door to see what was going on.

"Ack!" said the bald man, gripping the pillow with all his might. "Who the hell is THAT?"

Pete stood large as life in the doorway, grinning.

"No men," said Baldy. "I'm not paying for this. No way."

"You weren't paying for this anyways, cheap guy. It was a freebie, remember? Friend of the congressman and all?"

Baldy gulped. "I'm no friend of the congressman."

"And I'm no reporter," quipped Pete. "Except this here's my recorder." He pulled it out of a pocket.

"Stop that, Pete," I said. The poor naked guy was getting all red in the face and huffing like Thomas the Tank Engine.

But Pete was just getting started. "For the record, what's your name?"

Now the fat man went white.

"Bill," he said.

"Harry," said the blond.

"I'm getting outta here," the man muttered. I watched him scramble for clothes.

"Of course, this tape might easily be erased if we could come to some agreement."

We all looked at Pete with interest. Especially me.

"Shoes," he said.

"Shoes?"

He might as well have said purple octopuses.

Pete nodded, and indicated with a hand. "Those ones will do."

I wasn't surprised to see the stacked-heel pumps on the floor beside the bed.

"You want shoes?" Bill/Harry looked baffled.

Blondie came to life. "Don't you get it, Harry? They're shoe fetishists. They get off on fancy footwear." She looked dreamy. "I had a client once who would only do it if I wore Manolos. That was a great year."

"Take the damn shoes then. Take mine too—here. I got lots." Bill/Harry had a shoe in each hand, and it looked as if he was going to hand them over. I was wrong. He heaved them at me.

I screamed, and Pete yelled and launched himself across the room. He grabbed the fat man, and they both hit the floor. Blondie grasped the lamp on the bedside table and tried to whack him with it, but the cords wouldn't come loose and she ended up sprawled across the bed.

I was mesmerized. Those breasts couldn't be real.

"Help! Help! Help!" squeaked Bill/Harry.

"Get the shoes!" yelled Pete. He grappled with the sweaty naked man on the carpet, trying to hold him down without touching various icky parts.

"You're like a greased pig," muttered Pete, losing his grip.

I lunged for the shoes just as three goons burst through the door.

"Yikes!" said Blondie, diving off the side of the bed.

"Aaaaaagh!" screamed Baldy, making a dash for the covers.

Two of the goons were standard issue, solid as brick walls and probably just as smart. The other goon was huge, and he spoke first.

"Gina?"

I pushed disheveled hair out of my eyes.

"Joey?"

He grinned.

"You're looking good." He peered at my cleavage. "Like the outfit. Your uncle know you're doing this?"

"I'm not 'doing this.' I'm getting the shoes. See?" I pointed to the scattered shoes on the floor.

"Good girl. I'll take them now." He gestured with a big hand.

Blondie popped up from her perch beside the bed. "My, you're big." She eyed him up and down.

He took a look at her big ones and blushed bright red.

I pointed to the shoes. "You can have them. I don't care if I never see them again. Nothing but trouble from start to finish, and to top it off, they hurt like hell."

"Grab them, Harry!"

"Wha—?"

"The shoes! Grab the shoes! They must be valuable!"

There was a little *ting*, and then a sizzle, and the lights went out.

"What the fuck!"

Someone pushed by me and sent me sprawling. I landed on the floor on my butt, struggling for air.

There was a *thwack*, and a male voice went "ooof!" A body tripped over me and landed hard. I scooted backward on my butt until I hit a wall and then tried to keep out of range.

Someone hollered, "Get him!" There was crashing and swearing and pounding of feet. Blondie screamed, and then some guy yelped.

"Fucking bitch!"

More pounding feet in the hall. I waited. It got quiet.

Light was coming in from the hallway behind the open door. When my eyes adjusted to it, I looked around. I was alone in the room with the stolen shoes.

I stood up carefully, adjusted the bodice of my maid outfit and looked around.

Pete dashed in, breathing hard. "You all right?"

I pointed to the shoes.

"Shit," said Pete. "How did that happen?"

"I think they grabbed the man's shoes by mistake."

He shook his head. "Stupid git."

"You can't blame Joey. He didn't know what shoes, and we usually use men to carry. Tony was wearing men's shoes after all."

He sat down on the bed, cradling his right hand. It looked pretty mashed.

"So what do we do now?"

"We get out of here fast. With the shoes."

CHAPTER THIRTEEN

It was a slimy motel that had seen better times. In the '70s, it had seen better times. It was perfect. "Pull in," I said.

"What do you think?" Once inside, Pete glanced around doubtfully. Flocked velvet wallpaper was peeling behind the reception desk.

"No one would ever think of looking for me here." I was cheerful. "Get us rooms on the same floor if you can."

"Separate rooms?" He scratched his head. "We only had one room back at the posh hotel."

"I wasn't expecting to stay there overnight. This is different. It's only our first date," I said primly.

He had the grace to laugh. "First date—right. Never had a first date last twenty-four hours before. Or skipped across the border twice. Or had to fight off hookers and thugs. Not on a first date."

"Okay, our second date. And remember who my godfather is."

"Oh, I haven't forgotten," he said darkly.

Actually, I'm not a prude. And Pete is very, very yummy. Besides, he might have to marry me after this jaunt. But I had another motive for not sharing.

There was something I needed to do first. Alone.

I waited until after we parted, then took a quick cab from the motel to a nearby plaza. They were very helpful. After I had done my business, I scooted back. Time to shower and…what exactly?

I thought about all the men in my life. Sweet Terry from high school. A smattering of guys from university who went running after they figured out who I was. And—okay—a few unworthy males Uncle Vince and the boys sent running. Yes, I was a flirt, but for the "girl with the longest confession," I wasn't a slag. Even the blessed Virgin Mary would need only one hand to count the guys I'd been with.

This yearning I had for Pete went deep. The visual clues were all there, but it seemed to be triggered by his smell. This sensation was new to me. It was like hunger, only sweeter. The closer I got to him, the closer I wanted to get. I wanted— well, I wanted to follow it through... see where it would lead.

After the shower, I dressed again in the blue suit and white tank. Not so white, now. This outfit was getting grungy— a shopping trip was in order tomorrow.

But on it went, and out I went. Down the hall. Knocked on the door.

Pete opened it, wearing only a towel.

"Changed my mind," I said.

"We already paid for two rooms." He raised one eyebrow.

"I'm good for it."

He held the door wide, and I walked right in.

* * *

Next morning, reality hit.

"This place is really a hole." I was looking straight at the ceiling, trying not to look in the corners.

"Murrrph?"

"Darling, the places you take me. And on our first night together."

"First morning," Pete mumbled and reached for me.

"Oh no!" I gasped. "Not again. You can't be—"

"Yup." He covered my mouth with his own.

Sometime later, I woke up. I tried to sit up.

"Ouch!" This was a first. Too much activity for one night.

I heard a snicker.

"Easy for you to say! All you have to do is pee from yours. I have to sit on mine."

Now he laughed.

"And walk. I may never walk again," I mumbled, shuffling over to the edge of the bed.

"So don't try," Pete said, pulling me back.

* * *

It was lunchtime. I demanded food.

"There's a greasy spoon attached to this joint. Are you feeling brave?"

I whipped on my blue suit and tank. "Lemme at 'em."

Checking out took no time, as it involved throwing the key on the counter of the empty reception desk. And, of course, we had no luggage to pack.

"Can't imagine what people will think, us leaving here with no luggage," I said.

"They'll think we're like every other couple sneaking out of here with no luggage," quipped Pete. "And they'd be right."

I hit him with my purse.

The greasy spoon lived up to its billing. God, it smelled good. I plunked myself down on the red vinyl bench across from Pete.

"Hey, look here!" I pointed to the menu. "They have eggs Benedict."

Pete frowned. "You're going to risk hollandaise sauce in a place like this?"

"Done!" I said, putting the menu down. "And buckets of coffee."

The waiter was a skinny high-school kid with bad acne. The coffee was a blend of Colombian and old shoes.

"Ick." I pulled a face.

"I'll take you to Four-bucks later," Pete said.

The food came, and we leaped on it. We cleaned off our plates completely. Okay, maybe they had never been clean exactly, but they were free of major food groups. I leaned back on the plastic bench and sighed with contentment.

"How were your eggs and bacon?" I asked. I sipped more of the coffee and pulled a face.

"Better than the coffee," Pete said. He signaled for the bill.

I studied his face from across the booth. It was a nice face, I decided. Not movie-star handsome, exactly, but masculine with rugged planes. I could live with this face every morning.

Pete paid the bill, and we were off.

"So, first, gas for the car. Then—what exactly?" Pete walked briskly through the parking lot toward the rental car. I hurried along beside him, trying to keep up.

"Don't rush me," I said. "Good plans take time. But I'm thinking we catch a flight back to Toronto. That's probably the closest airport with a direct flight—*ooph!*"

They took us from behind. I saw Pete go down with a thug on his back. Someone with huge arms grabbed me around the waist and lifted me off the ground.

"Get her shoes!" Joey yelled.

"Joey, you son of a bitch, put me down!" I shrieked. I could hardly breathe, he was squishing me so hard.

Another goon—Bertoni—pulled at the shoes on my feet. I kicked him in the face. He yelped. "Bitch!"

I kicked him again.

"Stop squeezing me!" I yelled. I did not feel good.

Joey hollered, "Got 'em! Let's get out of here."

He dropped me, and I went *splat* on the pavement. Pete was just getting to his feet. Our assailants were already over to their van. They piled inside and pulled away.

"Are you okay?" Pete asked. He sounded concerned.

"I don't feel so well," I said. Then I lost the hollandaise.

* * *

It's a good man who will take care of you when you're throwing up. Pete was a good man. He held me so I didn't fall over, and then he found something to wipe my face.

"Well, that was a waste of seven bucks," he said.

I was more worried about being shoeless.

We found flip-flops in a dollar store around the corner. Luckily, they had a pair in my size. Pete didn't like the look of them much.

"How can you stand wearing those things?" he said while we were going through security at the airport.

"You should try wearing thong under-wear," I replied.

The flight back to Toronto was uneventful, which was a real treat for a change. As we were landing, Pete said, "Phoenix is nice. I'd like to see more of it. We should go back there sometime."

I nodded and smiled. That *we* had a good ring to it. This was encouraging. It signaled he wasn't planning to disappear as soon as we got off the plane. Which was a good thing, because we still had some-thing left to do.

CHAPTER FOURTEEN

It was a nice dream. We were at David's Shoes in posh Oakville, and Pete was buying me a pair of Manolos…

The phone rang. It wasn't the phone at David's Shoes. It was the phone in my condo. I picked it up and muttered "Hello."

"They want the body."

"What?" I cradled the phone to my chin.

"The body. They want it." Was that Sammy's voice, or was I still dreaming?

"What body?" I said. Still not awake. What time was it? I looked at the clock.

4:30 AM. I looked to the other side of the bed. I wasn't alone.

"Tony's. The body that's in the morgue. The guys in New York. They want it. We hafta get it to them. Vinnie wants it done now, before the morgue creeps dissect it. Angelo says it's on the schedule for this morning."

"Who is it?" Pete muttered. He lay on his back. His eyes weren't open yet.

"Sammy," I whispered.

"Gina, are you there?"

"I'm here," I said. "So they want the body. They can have it." I didn't want it.

A pause.

"Aren't there rules about things like that? Taking bodies across the border?" I asked.

"Not if nobody knows about it."

"I'm trying to figure out what this has to do with me."

"Vinnie said to call you on account of he has a high opinion of your brains."

So they needed a plan.

"Sammy, I'm a jeweler, not a criminal mastermind. Why do we have to do this under the table?"

"'Cause they want it now, not after the morgue creepies do their pulling-apart thing. They want the body intact. For burial."

I sighed. "And why do we care?"

"You wanna start a war?"

"I don't want to start anything! But why me? I didn't have anything to do with the shooting."

"They don't know that. You took 'im to the place, and he got nailed. Maybe they think we set it up."

I was out of the bed and pacing now. "That's nuts! I thought they got him plugged by his own people because he was out of control, or something."

"So did I. They're not sayin'. An' Vince don't wanna take the chance at starting bad relations, you know? So we're doin' this little favor for them. You gotta be involved so it's looks like we're doing this in good faith."

I counted to seven. I could refuse. Couldn't I? But then they would do the whole comedy routine over again. I could see it all. Sammy phoning. Then Vince phoning. Then Paulo, Luca…Angelo at the door with more coffee. Then Aunt Miriam. Brrrr…I shivered at Aunt Miriam. Did I want to deal with a corpse or Aunt Miriam?

Sometimes decisions come easy. I said, "Okay, where are we meeting?"

He told me, and I hung up.

Pete rolled over. "What was that all about?"

"Nothing. I just have to go steal a body."

CHAPTER FIFTEEN

First I had to peel Pete off the ceiling.

Then I made him coffee.

"Simple, really," I lied. "We get the body from the morgue and then we take it to Buffalo."

"What—on a shopping trip?"

This was going to take more explaining than I thought. Which was a problem.

"So I haven't worked out the details yet. But how much trouble can it be to smuggle one body over the border? I mean, really. People smuggle things all the time. Cigarettes...illegal handguns.

We smuggled a house-worth of jewels just the other day."

"And look where that got us!" Pete sounded a tad upset.

"You might say it got us into bed."

Pete didn't seem to see the humor.

I put my coffee cup down on the kitchen table. "It's okay, really. I've got a plan."

He stared at me and started shaking his head. "Oh no. Not another one of your 'plans.'"

"No, really! It's a very cunning plan." And it was.

I picked up the phone and punched numbers.

"Sammy, did Tony have his passport on him?"

Once I had the info, I spilled the details to Pete.

When I was done, he shook his head. "I must be nuts."

"It'll work!" I insisted. "We just have to act fast."

We were at the hospital by 5:00 AM. Hospitals never sleep, but morgues do. So do their occupants. Angelo was there to meet us, and he hustled us in.

"I got him good and cold," Angelo said. He swung open the compartment door and showed us the body.

"Thank God you dressed it! Angelo, you're a prince." A frozen wiener was the last thing I wanted to see. Especially a dead one.

"Here's a gurney," Angelo said. "I figure, we put him on the gurney, and then I help you get him to the car."

Pete looked skeptical. "Not that I want to throw water on this very clever plan, but what if he melts?"

"You drive like a bat out of hell to the border, and we got people waiting just over the bridge. One hour, tops. Use your air conditioning. He'll hold till then."

I certainly hoped so.

We got him to my car. Pete and Angelo worked to get the package formerly known as Tony into the backseat.

"Just lay him down on those pillows back there. And cover him with the blanket."

"He's frozen, Gina! His knees won't bend well," Pete said.

"We'll have to prop up his torso on the far side of the car to get his legs to fit in over here. Pile the pillows under him, and maybe when he melts a bit, he'll lean over onto them." Angelo was trying to be helpful.

They struggled to fit the "package" in the back. I started to have doubts about this plan.

But they managed it. Pete stood back and peered down at the body.

"Looks a bit gray," he said.

"He looks ghastly," I countered, "but then he would, after an all-night bachelor party at the Polecat Strip Club in Niagara Falls."

Pete groaned. "And who am I in all this deception?"

"You're my boyfriend."

"And who are you?"

"I'm his cousin."

"I thought you really were his cousin."

"I am. Well, I almost am," I said, thinking back to our whole cousin-in-law-through-marriage conversation. "That's why this plan is so good."

It wasn't really, but you have to celebrate the small things.

"I gotta be getting back to the morgue. Good luck," said Angelo. He practically ran back to the building.

"Okay, let's move it," I said to Pete.

"Why am I driving your car, again?" Pete started her up and shifted into drive.

"Because your car only has two seats."

Pete glanced over. "I meant, why aren't you driving?"

"Ah!" I said. "Well, that's the clever part of the plan." And I told him what I had in mind.

Pete sighed. "Tell me again why I'm doing this."

"Because you're crazy about me, and because the sex is amazing."

Now he laughed. "Maybe I'm just crazy. But I'm glad you think it's amazing."

Pete seemed pretty comfortable driving my car. We whipped through the streets of Steeltown and headed straight for the freeway. Next stop, Buffalo.

It would have been a good plan. I'm pretty sure it would have worked.

We almost got to Niagara Falls before the car broke down.

"Son of a bitch!" yelled Pete, pulling off to the shoulder.

Smoke billowed from under the hood.

I reached for my cell phone.

"Sammy, we got a problem." I explained the situation.

"Um, Gina? I think we should probably get out of the car."

I looked up. Flames were coming out of the hood now.

"Holy crap!" I pushed open the door and pitched myself out. "Yikes!"

The shoulder gave way to a steep ditch. I rolled into a mass of bulrushes.

Pete whacked the top of the hood with his jacket, trying to put out flames.

I crawled up the side of the bank on my hands and knees. Pete was still yelling and cursing. The flames shot three feet in the air.

"Well, at least they'll be able to find us easily," I said. This day was not going according to plan.

I found my cell phone at the side of the road. Sammy was still yelling out of it. I sat down and reassured him that we would live.

"But we have another problem," I said. "The package is melting."

CHAPTER SIXTEEN

When the ice-cream truck pulled up, I wasn't surprised to see Sammy get out. Another car pulled up behind it. A nice new red one with spiffy wheels and no flames shooting out from under the hood. My cousin Luca got out of it.

"Nice save," said Pete, admiring the freezer compartment of the truck.

I made introductions. "Sammy, Pete. Pete, Sammy."

Sammy moved forward to shake hands.

"Sorry we got you into this," Sammy said. Darn, I was proud of him. It was a nice sentiment. It might mean they weren't going to kill him.

Pete nodded. "Gina kinda dragged me into it."

"She can drag with the best of them."

I rolled my eyes. "And this is my cousin Luca," I said.

Luca was not tall, but he was built like a boxer, light on his feet and heavy with muscle. He was wearing all black, as usual. His long dark hair was tied back in a ponytail.

Not surprisingly, he managed a gym.

Luca glared at Pete. Didn't hold out his hand.

Pete took his cue from Luca's folded arms. He bobbed his head. "Howdy."

Luca nodded, then turned to me. "This the guy with the newspaper?"

"It's okay. He's been warned."

"Warn him again."

"No need," said Pete. "I'm sports beat, not crime. And I'm not stupid."

Luca looked Pete up and down, like a breeder looking over a stud horse. Then he stood back and nodded.

"You played for the Vikings. Quarterback. I saw the game they carried you off the field."

Pete nodded. He was clearly chuffed.

I was also impressed. Had someone been doing their homework? Or was Pete a more famous guy in the sports world than I had ever realized?

"Your first year in the pros."

Pete shrugged. "Wrecked my knee. That game finished my career."

Sammy nodded. "Gotta be tough to be a quarterback. Nerves of steel. They come at you from all directions."

Pete said nothing.

"You box?" Luca asked.

"Used to. College," Pete said. Well, there was another thing I didn't know.

Luca squinted. "Two twenty?"

"Thereabouts."

Luca turned to me then.

"Bring him down to the club sometime, Gina. We'll fit him up."

"Yeah, sure," I said. "But in the meantime, can you do something about this popsicle melting back here?"

"I got this, Gina," said Sammy. "You drive Luca's car back to Hamilton. We'll take it from here."

Relief! I felt relief. "Umm...what are you going to do?"

Sammy looked at me quizzically. "You really want to know?"

"No!" I yelped, hitting my forehead with a palm. "Nope. Don't tell me. I'm outta here. Say hi to Aunt Miriam."

"See you at dinner tomorrow. Bring the boyfriend."

"Sure," I tossed back. To Pete, I whispered, "Get in the car. And don't look back."

Pete jumped into the car. It was a sporty Japanese thing. The keys were in the ignition. He revved her up and booted it.

"Sure glad that's over." He sighed. "I'll turn around at the next exit."

"Umm...nope. Can't do that. We still have to go to Buffalo."

"What?"

My turn to suck in air. "It's about the stones."

Pete glared at me. "What about the stones?"

"Well...you may have been wondering what became of them."

Silence.

"I thought Joey got them when those goons attacked us in Phoenix. Weren't they in your shoes?"

"Em..." I hesitated. "Not exactly. Don't you remember? I was wearing flats."

Pete heaved a huge sigh. "Okay. What did you do with them?"

I told him.

"You WHAT?"

"It seemed a sensible thing! I was desperate. And you said nobody was living there right now."

Pete hit the steering wheel with the palm of his hand.

"I honestly didn't think you'd mind," I said. Okay, so that was a lie.

He pulled into the fast lane and stomped on the gas.

"I don't know why I'm doing this," he grumbled. "Why am I doing this again?"

It seemed a good idea to remind him. "Last night was amazing, remember? And then again at three AM."

"That is really low, bringing sex into it," he said.

I smiled sweetly. "Not to mention, you're sort of in this up to your neck. Not that I'd tell the cops on you or anything."

"Oh yeah." He snorted. "Thanks for that."

"Sorry. But you see, if you hadn't followed me to the bank machine—"

"I wasn't following you!"

"—then we never would have gone to Buffalo!"

"Or Phoenix. Or Toronto," he finished.

"And just think of everything you would have missed." I tried to pout, but I'm not really the pouting type.

"Remind me to call you Mata Hari."

"It's been done," I said mysteriously.

We got through the border with no problem at all. Of course, it's much easier to get through borders without a semi-frozen dead body pretending to be asleep in the backseat.

Half an hour later we pulled up in front of a stunning century-old home in Amherst. It had a wraparound porch, double front doors and beautiful gables. The thing had to be at least four stories high.

The flagstone sidewalk led up to the front steps. A well-tended flower garden lined it on both sides. The sort that's maintained by gardeners, if you know what I mean.

Pete switched off the engine.

"Honey, we're home," he quipped.

"Wow," I said. "Holy Toledo. Are your parents rich or something?"

Pete shrugged. "Dad is a cardiac surgeon. He's semi-retired now—uh—Gina, I think we have company."

I snapped my head around. A white panel van had pulled up behind us. Two thugs got out of the front seat and came running up alongside our car. I'd seen them before.

"Yikes!" I yelped. "Run!" I shoved open the door, vaulted out and thunked into a human wall.

"Oh, hi, Joey," I said. He looked pretty much the same as in Phoenix. Which is to say, big as a barn.

And pissed at me.

"Gina. How's things?"

"Same ol' same ol'," I said casually. "You?"

"Gimme the shoes, Gina."

"I don't have the shoes." This was true. I find it a relief to tell the truth every now and then.

"Of course you do."

"I don't, already! The postman has them."

"The what?"

"Don't believe her," said the second thug. "She's scamming you again."

I didn't like this goon. He was creepier than a zombie at Halloween and his hair was greasy.

"Shut up, Bertoni!" I yelled. "What do you know about classy shoes anyway? Your mother wears army boots!" Okay, so this was deteriorating somewhat.

"You mouthy bitch!"

I kicked him in the shins. He yelped.

Pete hauled me back out of reach.

"It's simple," he said calmly. "The shoes have been mailed back to Buffalo, by courier. They should arrive today. Any minute now. That's what we're waiting for."

"I wasn't planning to keep the rocks," I said to Joey. "I'm not crazy. I just wanted to get them off my hands before going back through customs. That's why I sent them here instead of Hamilton."

Joey shook his head. "You are a real screwup, you know."

"It's not my fault," I insisted. "The big blond from the hotel room stole my shoes when we were in the Galleria. We tracked her halfway across the States until you caught up with us in Phoenix."

"How could you lose a pair of shoes in a shopping mall? It was the whole reason you were going there!" Joey was clearly exasperated.

I didn't like his tone of voice. "I had a plan! It was a good plan too, and it would have worked if you and the goons hadn't barged into the hotel room. I would have given them to you right there, if you hadn't vamoosed outta the place. So it's *your* fault."

I was on a roll. "And besides"—I poked my finger into Joey's chest—"if you hadn't gone AWOL with that bar tart in Cheektowaga—"

"North Tonawanda."

"It can be frigging Timbuktu for all I care! The point is, *you* messed up the drop. And I'm called in to clean up, as usual." I stamped my foot like a five-year-old.

"So this is what you call cleaning up a mess? What we've been through?" Pete laughed.

There was dead silence.

I threw Pete a withering glance. Whose side was he on? That was it. I was outta here. They could all play together in the sandbox. They could beat each other silly, for all I cared. I held my head up high and made the announcement.

"I'm going home." I turned to Pete. "You can stay with these bozos and sign for the package."

"Wait a minute!" Pete said. "It's your package—you and the cousins, or whoever they are."

"Too bad," I shot back over my shoulder. "It's your business now. Your name is on the parcel. And this is your house." Well, not exactly—but it sure wasn't mine.

There was only one problem. My purse was still in the car. Which meant, so was my passport. Even worse, I wasn't going to get very far, because Pete had the car keys.

I turned back.

"Give me the keys," I said, trying to look tough.

"No way. Gina, be reasonable." Pete pleaded with both arms.

"Then I'll hitchhike." Sometimes I can be stubborn. Okay, make that childish.

"Uncle Vince will kill you if you hitchhike," said Joey. "It's dangerous."

"Right. And hanging out with you morons isn't?"

"Who are you calling a moron?" Bertoni looked threatening.

"Stay away from her," Pete growled. "She's with me."

"You and whose army, tough guy?"

Bertoni was about six inches shorter than Pete. He poked a finger into Pete's stomach. Pete socked him with a left hook. *Crunch!* Bertoni came back at him like a steamroller, and the two hit the ground in a wrestling clench.

"Kill him!" I yelled to Pete, with all the class of a gangster moll. "Kill the bastard!" I was jumping up and down, out of reach.

This was turning into a first-class street brawl. Pete shoved his huge hand against Bertoni's face. Bertoni got in a really good jab.

"Dammit!" Pete was going to have a killer black eye in the morning. They separated for a moment. Bertoni stumbled to his feet, and I saw my chance.

I looked around for anything that could be used as a weapon and saw the petunias lining the walkway. I pulled a plant out and threw it at Bertoni. That didn't work well. So I pulled a large geranium out of the ground with both hands and started to whack him with the root end. Dirt went flying everywhere.

"What the fuck are you doing?" he yelled. He reached up to rub his eyes, and Pete rushed him, taking him down in a football tackle. I frantically looked around for more weapons, but the impatiens were too small and the dusty miller looked limp.

Pete and Bertoni were still going at it, rolling over and over on the ground, crushing the phlox and petunias beneath them. They were headed for the rose-bushes when I heard the squeak of a faucet and a hiss. Joey calmly turned the hose on them.

"Shit!"

"Holy crap, that's cold!"

Then he turned it on me.

"Joey, you son of a bitch!" I shrieked. I still had the geranium in my hand, so I threw it at him. Then I charged right at him, taking the stream of water in the face.

"Give that to me," I screamed.

Joey swung around to deflect me. I leaped on his back, wrapping both legs around his waist. He hollered, but I locked my arms around his head and he couldn't see. We swung around glued together like a rodeo cowboy on the back of a bucking bronco in a really bad western. Round and round we lurched, me holding on like a boa constrictor, and Joey trying to tear my arms off his head. Water sprayed in every direction. I tried to grab the hose out of his hand, but his arm was too long.

None of us noticed the courier truck pull up behind our line of vehicles.

"Excuse me. Is anyone here called Pete Malone?"

"I am!" Four of us said in unison.

I slid down Joey's back and landed with a thump on the ground.

"He is!" I said and pointed at Pete.

"I have a parcel—"

"I'll take that!" said Joey. He reached for it.

"NO!" said the delivery man, pulling it away. "I can only give it to Pete Malone."

"I'm Pete." Pete stood up, dripping wet. Mud streaked his shirt. A pink petunia stuck in the side of his hair.

"He is too," I said. "I swear it." Not that my word was worth anything. I pushed myself to my feet.

"May I see your ID, sir?"

Pete stuck his hand in the back pocket of his pants and came out with a soggy wallet. He flipped it open.

"Here you go, sir." The delivery guy handed the parcel to Pete, who handed it to me. I handed it to Joey.

The delivery guy looked at all of us and shook his head. "Have a nice day." He turned and walked back to the van, still shaking his head.

Joey opened the box.

"The shoes!" he said. "Finally."

I peered over his shoulders. "Those are the ones. The rocks are in the heel. Heels from hell. You can keep them. Are we done here now?"

Joey nodded. His phone rang, and he pulled it from a pocket. He listened, and then his brow furrowed.

"Anything wrong?" I asked.

"For some reason, I have to go meet an ice-cream truck over by D'Youville. Who do we know that's got an ice-cream truck?"

Oops. No way I wanted to get involved in that again. Time to vamoose.

I walked over to the car, reached in for my purse and took out my cell phone. I punched in numbers.

"Mission accomplished," I said into the phone.

"The rocks are where they belong?"

"Sammy, what is the point of me being obscure if you are going to spell it all out?" Jeesh, sometimes I wonder if anyone in my family is cut out for this line of work.

"Good job, Gina. Is paperboy still with you?"

"His name is Pete," I reminded him.

"Got that. Sweetheart, you are going to marry the guy, right? And bring him into the family?"

"Um…that's a good question. A really good one. Yup, I'd say it's a doozie." I could feel the heat rising up my face.

"'Cause he really has to be part of the family now. We don't want to hafta whack the guy, you know?"

I gave a little strangled laugh.

Pete poked me in the arm.

"What does he want to know?"

I covered the cell phone speaker with my hand.

"He wants to know if you're going to marry me."

Pete grabbed the phone from me.

"Hello, Sammy. The answer is yes."

I stared at him with my mouth open, water dripping down my hair and onto my neck.

"Of course I know what I'm getting into. She's a nutcase," Pete said into the speaker. "Oh. You meant the family."

"Give it to me! Give it to me! Give it—" I tried to yank it out of his hand, but he held it up above my head.

"Sorry, Sammy, I have to go now. We both need to dry off. See you soon." He clicked off and handed it back to me. Then he reached forward with both arms and gathered me up in a wet embrace.

"You're crazy to get involved with me." My voice sounded muffled.

Pete kissed the top of my soggy head. "I'm crazy all right. Crazy about you."

I raised my face and looked into his eyes. Nobody would be whacking anyone, if I could help it.

"You don't know how relieved I am to hear that," I said. And I smiled.

MELODIE CAMPBELL has been a banker, marketing director, college instructor, comedy writer and possibly the worst runway model ever. Her work has appeared in *Alfred Hitchcock Mystery Magazine, Star Magazine, Flash Fiction, Canadian Living, Toronto Star, The Globe and Mail* and many more. *The Goddaughter* is Melodie's third published novel.

Titles in the Series

RAPID READS
